For Izzy, with love – S.P.
For Cat-Bear, who flew away – C.G.

The Day the Baby Blew Away © Frances Lincoln Limited 2004
Text copyright © Simon Puttock 2004
Illustrations copyright © Cathy Gale 2004
The right of Simon Puttock to be identified as the Author and Cathy Gale to be identified
as the Illustrator of this work has been asserted by them in accordance
with the Copyright, Designs and Patents Act, 1988

First published in Great Britain in 2004 by Frances Lincoln Children's Books,
4 Torriano Mews, Torriano Avenue, London NW5 2RZ

www.franceslincoln.com

Distributed in the USA by Publishers Group West

ISBN 1-84507-046-1

Printed in China

1 3 5 7 9 8 6 4 2

THE DAY THE BABY BLEW Away

Simon Puttock

Illustrated by
Cathy Gale

FRANCES LINCOLN CHILDREN'S BOOKS

Mama and Papa were hanging out washing,
the day the baby blew away.
The wind was whipping the dripping sheets
and the baby was fast asleep in the shade.

"Oh," sighed the wind, when it spied the baby.
"Oh, what curly fingers, oh, what tiny toes!
Oh, her hair blows thistledowny, gently to and fro.
I WANT that baby for my very own!"
And when Mama and Papa's backs were turned,
the wind...

...STOLE the baby!

"Hey!" cried Mama.

"Help!" cried Papa. "Put our baby down!"
But the wind just laughed a gusty laugh,
and headed into town.

And the baby, wildly sailing through the air,
woke up and started wailing.
"Hush-a-bye Baby," sang the wind.
"Hush-a-bye baby, sleep, sleep-o!"
But the baby would not hush,
and she would not sleep, oh no.
She wailed all the way down...

"Oh, what's the matter?" the wind asked the baby.
The baby only answered, "WAH!"
"I think," said the wind, "that I understand.
You're cold, that's what you are.
But I spy something to keep you warm.
I spy Mrs McGinty's shawl."

Down flew the wind, with the baby shrieking,
and Mrs McGinty felt fingers tweaking.
She wrapped her shawl tight, tighter round.
But the wind was too strong,
and her shawl was gone,
whirling and twirling above the town.

WwwaAaaaAAAAAAAAA hHhHH

"STOP, THIEF!" Mrs McGinty yelled.
"Bring back that baby and my shawl as well!"
And all the people passing by
heard Mrs McGinty and the baby cry.
"Stop!" they shouted. "Stop right now,
you great big thieving bully bluster!"

But the wind kept going
and the wind kept blowing,
faster and faster and faster,
and they ALL went chasing after,
through the streets and round the town,
and still the baby howled and howled.
Louder and louder, redder and redder,
crosser and crosser and crosser.

Grandpa was snoozing in his garden in the sun.
The wind and the baby woke him up.

WwwaAaaAAAAAAAAAAhHHhHH

"Hey!" he cried, "you great big snorter!
What are you doing with my granddaughter?
Give her back or there'll be trouble!
Put her down here at the double!"
But the wind said, "NO!" with a great big shout.

"OH-HO!" said Grandpa,
"then you'd better watch out!"
And he fetched his lasso from the shed
and WHIRLED and WHIRLED it round his head
and he caught the wind, and the baby too.

He pulled and hauled
and heaved and tugged them
right down to the ground.
The wind was well and truly caught,
and the baby was safe and sound.

Beautifully

But Grandpa was cross as cross can be.
He tied the wind in a prickle-pine tree.
"Don't you know better than to steal a baby?
Don't you know better than to cause so much worry?
You can stay up there until you're properly sorry!"

Mama and Papa and all the town,
huffing and panting and out of breath,
arrived to find the baby safe,
and Mrs McGinty's shawl as well.
"Our baby!" cried Mama and Papa.
"The baby!" cried everyone else.
"My shawl!" cried Mrs McGinty,
getting back her breath.

And they all sat down to have a rest,
and cups of tea were handed round,
while the wind sat high in the prickle-pine tree
and sulked in the prickle-pine boughs.

The wind blew hot, and the wind blew cold,
"I do NOT want to do as I am told,
but... oh," it sighed, "I'm all alone,
while everyone else is down below,
tickling the baby and having fun."
And the wind...

So the wind came down for a saucer of tea,
and rocked the baby sensibly.
It wasn't a wicked wind really, at all.
In fact, it soon made friends.

And when the baby was sleeping,
and everyone had to go,
by special request and to make amends,
the wind got up a great big BLOW
and very, very gently, it blew

EVERYONE
back home again.